E
MCG

McGovern, Ann

Scram kid!

DATE			
SEP 27	MAY 15	MAY 09 2007	
SEP 30	DEC 20	DEC 06 2007	
OCT 15	OCT 22		
NOV 18	APR 25		
DEC 16	FEB 22	SEP	
FEB 2	OCT 12	NOV 15	
MAR 18	DEC 24		
MAY 25			
MAR 23	DEC 4		
APR 6	FEB 28 2006		
MAR 10	NOV 02 2006		
MAY 7			

2118

© THE BAKER & TAYLOR CO.

SCRAM, KID!

Ann McGovern

ILLUSTRATED BY **Nola Langner**

THE VIKING PRESS   NEW YORK

First Edition. Copyright © 1974 by Ann McGovern. Illustrations copyright © 1974 by Nola Langner. All rights reserved. First published in 1974 by The Viking Press, Inc. 625 Madison Avenue, New York, N.Y. 10022. Published simultaneously in Canada by The Macmillan Company of Canada Limited. Printed in U.S.A. • Library of Congress Cataloging in Publication Data. McGovern, Ann. Scram, kid! Summary: In his frustration at being left out of the baseball game a young boy imagines some strange and funny things. 1. Baseball—Fiction. 2. City and town life—Fiction. I. Langner, Nola, illus. II. Title. PZ7.M1687Sc [E] 73—20017. ISBN 0—670—62370—9. 1 2 3 4 5 78 77 76 75 74

For Janet, with love · For Eli, with love

Sailing boats.
Running around.
Climbing trees.

Eating ice cream.
Playing baseball.

In the city, where Joe lives,
there are different things to do
on different Saturday mornings in the park.

Of all the things to do,
Joe wanted to play baseball more than anything else.
There were lots of kids playing baseball in the park,
but Joe didn't know any of them.

"Can I play?" Joe asked one of the boys.

"Scram, kid," said the boy, not even looking at Joe.

"We've got enough guys."

But Joe didn't want
to scram.
He wanted to play.
And then he got mad.

"GO FLY A KITE," Joe muttered,
clenching his fists and closing his eyes.
And, in the middle of the park,
Joe had a wide-awake dream.

It was a few minutes later, and Joe had cooled down.

"Can I play?" he asked another boy.

"I'll trade you my trading cards."

"Scram, kid," said the boy.

Joe didn't want to scram any more than he did before.

He wanted to play.

And he got mad
all over again.

"GO JUMP IN THE LAKE!"
Joe yelled.

"GET LOST!"
Joe shouted.

"GO SOAK YOUR HEAD!"
Joe screamed.

One of the boys was rounding third base.
He tripped. He fell. He was out!
Huh. I could have made that easy, Joe thought.

"Now can I play?" he asked the team captain.

"Scram, kid," said the captain.

"We don't need you."

"I'm better than all of you,"
Joe muttered.

"MAKE LIKE A DRUM
AND BEAT IT,"
Joe yelled.

"PUT THAT IN YOUR PIPE
AND SMOKE IT!"

"Wait till my friends come,"
Joe mumbled.
"WE'LL FIX THEIR WAGON!"

"Who needs them anyway?" Joe said,
looking at the kids to see if there were one—
just one—who might not be so awfully mean.

"Hey, please can I play, please?" Joe asked a boy
who looked as if he could be nice if he wanted to be.

But the boy didn't want to be.
"You don't even have a bat," the boy said.

"BATS!" said Joe.
"I have a million bats
at home," he muttered.

"BATS TO YOU!"

he screamed.

Then Joe walked
to a different part
of the park.

He saw a boy
carrying a small boat.

"I'm going to sail my boat
in the lake," the boy said.
"Can I sail it with you?" Joe asked.
"Sure, kid," said the boy.

Sailing boats.
Running around.
Climbing trees.

Eating ice cream.

Sometimes playing baseball.

And sometimes not.

There are different things to do
on different Saturday mornings

in the city, where Joe lives.

There sure are.

ANN McGOVERN and NOLA LANGNER have been friends since child-hood. Both grew up in New York City and share a sense of the diffi-culties of coping with the sometimes harsh experience of city life.

Ann McGovern has worked for a number of years in a variety of publishing jobs, from copywriter to book club editor, and has written twenty-five books for children. She and her husband live in Pleasant-ville, New York, but their enthusiasm for scuba diving often takes them and their four children to the coral reefs of the Caribbean.

Nola Langner began her career as an illustrator in a television studio. She has illustrated more than twenty books for children, four of which she also wrote. Ms. Langner has also traveled widely with her husband and their five children, most recently to Africa, which is the setting for a new book.